Honey's New Friend

For anyone who has ever
wanted a kitten – SM

ISBN 978-0-545-51085-1

Text copyright © 2011 by Sue Mongredien
Illustrations copyright © 2011 by Artful Doodlers
Photographs copyright © 2011 by iStockphoto.com

12 11 10 9 8 7 6 5 4 3 2 1   12 13 14 15 16 17/0

Printed in the U.S.A.   40
First Scholastic printing, October 2012

Sue Mongredien

Honey's New Friend

Scholastic Inc.

Meet the Kitten Club girls!

Amy
& Ginger

Mia
& Smokey

Molly
& Truffle

Ella
& Honey

Ruby
& Ziggy

Lily
& Buster

Chapter I

Ella Hughes was perched on the living room windowsill, eagerly gazing out at the street. It was Saturday afternoon, which meant only one thing: Kitten Club! Today's meeting was at Ella's house, and her friends were due to get there any minute. She smiled to herself, thinking about the surprise she and her mom had planned for the Kitten Club girls.

They were going to love it!

Their district also had no school for the entire next week, which Ella was very excited about. She was really looking forward to some fun-filled days with her mischievous kitten, Honey. And Grandma was coming to stay, too! It was going to be perfect.

Something suddenly tickled her bare feet, and she glanced down to see Honey jumping up at her toes.

"Hey," she said, hopping down to scoop her up. "Are you excited about Kitten Club, too? Who do you think will get here first?"

Honey made a sound that was half meow, half purr as Ella petted her. Then she spotted a fly buzzing around in the corner of the windowsill. She wriggled free of Ella's arms and scampered over to pounce on it. Ella smiled. Honey wasn't the type of kitten who would sit still and be cuddled forever—she wanted to play all day!

Then Honey caught sight of Misty, the family's other cat, curled up fast asleep on the sofa. The sofa was just within leaping distance of the windowsill, and Honey crouched low, quivering with excitement, her eyes fixed on the dozing older cat.

Just in time, Ella realized what her lively kitten was planning. "Oh, no you don't," she said, and grabbed hold of Honey quickly. "Jumping on Misty is *not* a good idea!" she added, petting her kitten's soft little head.

Honey gazed up at Ella with her big green eyes, as if the thought had never crossed her mind. Ella giggled. Honey really was a troublemaker sometimes, and loved pouncing on Misty's tail or chasing after her. Honey was just being playful—she was only a kitten, after all—but Misty would get very angry at being woken up or leaped on, and would sometimes lash out or growl at Honey. In fact, Ella thought as Honey jumped out of her arms in pursuit of the buzzing fly again, it was a miracle that her kitten and cat were in the same room together without a fight breaking out yet.

Just then, Ella caught sight of Mia walking up the sidewalk with her dad, and waved excitedly through the window at her. Oh, and there was Molly's mom's car, dropping off Molly, Ruby, and Lily, too. Ella picked up Honey and rushed to open the front door. Kitten Club was about to begin—hooray!

"Hi, everyone!" Ella said as her friends trooped into the house. "Oh, is that Amy's car pulling up, too? Wonderful! We're all here."

The six girls had met back in the summer, when they were each choosing kittens from Chestnut Farm. They'd all really hit it off, so Lily had suggested forming a club together . . . and Kitten Club had begun!

"Hi, Ella, hi, Honey," Mia said, hanging up her coat. "Brrr, it's cold out there today."

"It just started to rain, too," Amy said, taking off her boots and standing them neatly by the wall. "Hi, everyone! Hello, Honey—what a wriggler you are!"

Ella laughed. "I think she's impatient to get Kitten Club started," she said. "Should we head to the living room? I set everything up in there."

She led them in. Ella had spread some cushions on the floor, and brought down her beanbag from her bedroom so that everyone could gather around the Kitten Club scrapbook. Earlier, her dad had helped her make a tray of drinks for everyone, and they'd also put out some mini muffins and red grapes on a plate.

"Oh, we've got Misty *and* Honey in with us today," Lily said, walking over to where Misty was still fast asleep. She petted her gently and Misty opened her eyes a crack, then shut them again.

"Hello, Misty," said Molly, going over to pet her, too. She smiled. "Doesn't she look big? You get so used to having a dinky little kitten that grown-up cats seem like giants all of a sudden."

"I kept thinking that when we first got Honey," Ella agreed, putting Honey down on the carpet. "Misty's paws suddenly seemed as big as shovels next to Honey's tiny ones." She grinned as her kitten wandered over to Ruby, who was sitting on the floor

nearby, and started batting interestedly at
the beaded bracelet on her wrist. "Watch out,
Rubes, kitten alert!"

Ruby giggled and petted Honey. "Hey you,
that's a bracelet, not a cat toy," she said.

The girls sat in a circle on the floor, and
Ella passed around the plate of muffins.

"Yum," said Amy, biting into a chocolate
one. "Should we get started? Where's
our scrapbook?"

Ruby produced it from her bag and opened
it up on her lap. "It's getting really full," she
said, flicking through the pages they'd already
filled. Every week, the girls wrote in all their
kitten news, and stuck in any photos or
pictures. A lot had happened since their first
meeting back in the summer!

Ruby found the next empty page and

neatly wrote the date. "Okay, time for our roll call," she said with a grin. "Tomboy?"

"Meow!" said Ella, answering to her secret club nickname.

"Witch Cat?"

"Meoooow!" yowled Mia, making a spooky face, which made everyone laugh.

"Alley Cat?"

"Meow-oh!" said Molly, jumping as Honey attacked the hem of her jeans.

"Scatterbrain?"

"MEOW!" replied Lily dramatically, holding up her hands like paws. Both Misty and Honey turned to stare at her in surprise for a moment, and everyone burst into giggles. Lily was *so* going to be on the stage when she was grown up, Ella thought to herself with a grin. Misty blinked, and then settled back down to sleep.

"Green Eyes," Ruby said.

"Meow," Amy replied.

"And Glamour-Puss—that's me," Ruby said, ticking herself off. "Let's get this meeting started! What's everyone's news this week?"

"Well," Molly began, but before she could say anything else, Finn, Ella's twin brother, burst into the room with his friend Lucas.

"I'm *so* going to beat you," Finn said to Lucas as he switched on the TV and the PlayStation, ignoring the girls. "I've been practicing a ton for this. Bring it on!"

Ella bristled. Finn was such a pain! Couldn't he see that they were using the living room? "Hey, we're having a meeting," she said. "Go and play somewhere else."

The TV blared thunderous music as the

boys' game began loading. Finn ignored Ella and tossed one of the game controllers to Lucas, taking the other for himself. Then they both sat on the sofa, making Misty's ears prick up in annoyance.

"Finn!" Ella said. "I'm talking to you!"

"Yeah, yeah," he said. "Whatever."

"Welcome to . . . JUNGLE WARS!" boomed a deep voice from the TV. "Prepare for battle."

Finn snickered as Honey bounded across the room and leaped onto his feet. "Welcome to . . . CAT WARS!" he said, picking up Honey and whizzing her through the air.

"Finn, *don't*!" Ella cried, jumping up in alarm.

"Prepare for battle," Finn said, and

plopped Honey right onto Misty's back.

Misty yowled and lashed out angrily at Honey, who almost fell off the sofa in her hurry to run away. Both boys burst into guffaws.

Ella picked up Honey and cradled her,

feeling furious with her brother. "You could have hurt Honey doing that. And now you've upset Misty, too, when I'm already having trouble trying to help Misty and Honey be friends. Good work," she snapped sarcastically. She turned to her friends, still prickly with rage. "Come on, girls, let's go upstairs, away from these boneheads."

"Whatever!" called Finn in an irritating singsong voice as they left the room.

Ella stalked upstairs, clutching Honey to her chest. "Boys!" she muttered.

Chapter 2

Up in her bedroom, Ella took a while to calm down. "My brother is so annoying!" she fumed, her fingers trembling as she petted Honey. "Why does he have to stir up trouble like that? It drives me crazy!"

"Boys are big pains," said Molly, who had three brothers of her own. She put an arm around Ella, and they both petted Honey for

a minute. Mia passed Ella her drink, which she'd brought up for her, and Ruby, who'd remembered to bring the plate of muffins, handed them around again.

"Thanks, guys," Ella said, her anger draining away. "Let's try again. What's everybody's news?"

The club members swapped stories about their kittens, and wrote them in the scrapbook. "How about you, Tomboy?" Amy said after a while. "What have you and Honey been up to this week?"

"Well, for most of it I've been trying to stop this little minx from fighting with Misty," she replied, tickling Honey under the chin. "Poor Honey just wants to play, but Misty likes sleeping for hours and hours and Honey gets on her nerves. It's really tricky."

Lily looked thoughtful. "You know . . .
when Jessica was born, I wasn't all that
happy about her at first," she said. "It
seemed like Mom and Dad gave her all the
attention, and I felt like they didn't love me
as much as her." She shrugged. "Now I
know that really they love us both the same.

But what I'm trying to say is that maybe Misty needs some extra TLC, so that she knows *she's* still loved."

"That's a good idea," Ella said. "Maybe we *have* given Misty less attention since Honey's come to live with us. I'll be extra nice to her this week."

"You could try putting a bell on Honey's collar, too," Ruby suggested. "We've got one on Ziggy's collar so that the birds will hear him out in the yard and know to fly away. And if Honey's jingling around the place, it'll give Misty some warning that there's a kitten nearby."

"That's another good idea," Ella said, feeling more cheerful. "Thanks, guys. I'll try both of those things. Hopefully they'll help with the problem."

There was a knock on the door just then, and Ella's mom popped her head into the room. "Hello, everyone," she said. "Sorry I didn't say hello earlier, but I only just got back from work. Ella, I'm ready to do the You-Know-Whats when you are."

Ella smiled. She'd been so mad with her brother, she'd almost forgotten about the surprise she and her mom had planned for the others. "Oh, yes," she said. "Thanks, Mom. We'll do it now. Come on, everyone. Downstairs again!"

"What's happening? Where are we going?" Mia asked, jumping off Ella's bed.

"Hmm. . ." Ella said mysteriously as she led them back downstairs. "Wait and see."

Ella and her mom took the girls into the kitchen, where the table had been covered with newspaper, and lots of different colors of paint had been set out. Ella's friends gave an "Ooooh!" of excitement, and her mom smiled.

"I don't know if Ella's told you, but I run the pottery-painting café in town," she said. "And we thought it might be a nice idea if we had our own Kitten Club pottery-painting session here at home. I brought you each a door plaque to decorate, and we have lots of different paint colors. I'll fire the plaques for you during the week, and Ella will bring them to your next meeting. How does that sound?"

"That sounds totally cool!" Mia said happily. She loved drawing and painting. "Thank you so much!"

"Great," Amy said, her eyes shining. "What a fabulous idea!"

The girls sat around the table and began to paint. Ruby chose a pink background for her door plaque, then painted "Kitten Lover" on it in swirly silver letters. Molly painted stripes on hers, with "Molly's Bedroom" and a row of kitten-sized paw prints along the bottom. Ella painted her plaque blue, with "No Boys Allowed" in big letters.

They chatted as they painted, while Honey crazily chased a Ping-Pong ball around their feet, making the girls giggle whenever she brushed past them. "So what are you all up to over our school break?" Lily asked, dipping her paintbrush into the gold paint. "Tomorrow we're going to stay with my grandma and grandpa for a few days," she continued. "Our neighbors are taking care of Buster while we're gone—they've promised to cuddle and play with him a lot, but I'm going to miss him so much." She made an anguished face and Ella smiled to herself. Lily was always such a drama queen!

"My cousins are coming to stay," Mia said, carefully adding a purple swirl to her plaque. "They're really fun—and Mom said they're dying to meet Smokey."

"And it's Halloween at the end of the week, too, isn't it?" Molly said. "I can't wait. I love Halloween." An excited look came over her face. "Hey! We should have a Halloween party at our next Kitten Club meeting! I'm sure my mom will say it's okay to have it at our house."

"Ooh, yes," Ella said at once. "We could all wear costumes. Awesome!"

"I bet Grandma will help you with a costume," Ella's mom said, overhearing their conversation. "She's really good at making things."

Ella smiled. "That's a great idea."

"And we can play Halloween games at the party," Amy put in enthusiastically. "Ooh, and tell spooky ghost stories, too!"

As the girls discussed a Halloween

Kitten Club and all the fun things they could do together, Misty slunk into the kitchen, looking like she'd had quite enough of the boys' noise. Honey made an excited leap toward her, startling the older cat. Misty hissed, her tail fluffing up like a bottle brush, then scuttled out through the cat flap. It was still raining outside, and she took shelter under a bush, looking thoroughly miserable.

"Poor old Misty," Ella said, watching her.

It was awful that Misty preferred sitting out in the rain to being in the house with Honey. She made a vow then and there that her project was to make Misty feel happier, and to persuade the two cats to be friends. She would brush Misty's long gray fur every day and find something extra yummy for the old cat to have for dinner. Project Happy Cats would start right away!

Chapter 3

That evening at dinner, Ella told her family
her plans for keeping the peace between
the two cats, and hopefully building a
friendship. Her mom nodded. "That all
sounds very sensible," she said. "Since you
have a week off from school, you should have
more time to play with Honey, which means
she won't be bothering Misty all the time."

"I'll go to the pet store tomorrow and pick up a collar with a bell on it," Dad added. "It will give us all a little warning that Honey's in the area. She pounced on my foot earlier, and I almost fell over, I was so startled!"

Finn had been quiet throughout this conversation, and Ella pointed her fork at him. "And no more cat wars, Finn," she said shortly. "That just makes everything ten times worse."

"Yeah, yeah, whatever," Finn said, making a face. "Honestly—girls!"

SUNDAY

Started Project Happy Cats today! Dad got Honey a new collar with a bell on it, and she now jingles and jangles wherever she goes—every time she hears it, Misty's ears prick up and she runs off. Still, it's better than them fighting all the time, I guess!

I spent a long time playing with Honey today—it was so fun. I made some tunnels for her out of old newspaper and she loved going through them . . . and then attacking the newspaper and ripping it to shreds! She had her crazy face on—it really made me laugh.

crazy!

Then she was worn out and fell asleep on my bed, so I went and gave Misty a nice long grooming session, brushing her coat over and over. She purred and purred.

Grandma's going to be here in the morning—I can't wait to introduce her to Honey!

Ding-dong!

"Could you get that, Ella?" her mom called. "I'm on the phone."

"Sure," Ella said, scrambling off the sofa where she'd been playing with Honey. She ran to the front door, opened it, and beamed. "Grandma!" she said happily, throwing her arms around her.

Grandma gave Ella a big squeeze. She smelled like lavender and peppermints, and always gave the best hugs. "Hello, sweetheart," she said. "It's lovely to see you. I thought of all sorts of fun things we can do together while I'm here . . . and I brought my bag of tricks, too!"

Ella smiled. Grandma was one of those people who was constantly busy and who never sat still. She couldn't even watch

TV without knitting or sewing or working on a tapestry. Her "bag of tricks" was always full of arts and crafts supplies, and there was usually some cool stuff in there, like unusually shaped buttons, tons of bright embroidery thread, or pieces of beautiful fabric. "Sounds good to me," Ella said happily. "Do you think there might be something in your bag of tricks that I could use for a Halloween costume?"

Grandma's eyes twinkled. "I'm sure we can find something spooky in there," she said. "Now, where's this kitten of yours? I've been dying to meet her!"

Ella took Grandma through to the living room, but just as they walked in, both Honey and Misty shot out. Misty looked thoroughly fed up as she tried to escape from Honey, who was chasing after her, frantically trying to pounce on Misty's tail.

"Oh, Honey!" sighed Ella, running after her kitten and making a grab for her. Misty shot outside, where it had just started drizzling. Ella gave Grandma a sad smile. "As you can see, Honey and Misty aren't getting along very well, but I'm working on it."

Ella's mom came in then, and Finn shuffled in to say hello, and soon after that it was time for lunch. Poor Misty stayed out in the rain the whole time, and Ella felt terrible. She had to try harder with Project Happy Cats!

WEDNESDAY

It has been raining nonstop since Monday—
arrgh! Grandma took us to the movies
yesterday, and we went swimming this morning, but
the rest of the time we've been cooped up indoors.
Finn is driving me nuts, moaning
about how bored he is.

Grandma had some black
crêpe paper in her bag, so we
made a cardboard witch's hat
then covered it with the crêpe
paper. I stuck silver moons and
stars on it, too, and it looks really cool.
She said we can pick up some sparkly black fabric
for a dress and cape next time we go into town.
If the rain ever stops!

This afternoon, we made cookies with Grandma,
but Finn got annoyed and threw a
handful of flour at me when I told him
to stop stealing the chocolate chips.

Then Grandma scolded him, and he went off in a huff, and THEN we heard him shout "Cat wars!" and start a fight again with Honey and Misty. I could've killed him!

Even worse, when I tried to break up the fight, I got scratched by Misty. OW. It still really hurts. It's all my stupid brother's fault!

One good thing is that Misty really likes Grandma. She cuddles up on her lap every evening, purring and purring, while I keep Honey distracted by playing with her. So Grandma is helping with Project Happy Cats, even if Finn isn't!

On Thursday, the rain stopped, so Grandma took Ella and Finn to the playground, where they bumped into some friends from school. Then, on Friday, they finally went shopping, and Grandma took Ella into a shop that sold lots of different fabrics. Ella found one that was black with tiny golden stars scattered throughout. She held up the roll, beaming. "Look! This will be perfect for my witch's costume!" she said.

"A witch sounds about right," Finn muttered, earning himself a kick from Ella. "Ow! Grandma, she kicked me!"

Grandma rolled her eyes and laughed. "As well as a witch dress, we need some witch *magic* to stop you two from arguing," she said. "Honestly!"

Once they got home, Grandma measured Ella and drew out a pattern on the black material. Ella helped cut the material to the right shape, and chose a large midnight-black button from Grandma's bag that would be perfect for holding the cape together.

"You're going to be the best-dressed witch there has ever been," Grandma said with a wink as she threaded her needle.

Ella hugged her. "You're the best *grandma* there has ever been," she said, feeling excited about her costume.

Later that day, Ella went over to Amy's house. It felt good to get away from her brother for a while. Amy was fairly new to the area, but both girls had horseback-riding lessons together on the weekends, and Ella had enjoyed getting to know her. And her marmalade-colored kitten, Ginger, was absolutely adorable, too!

"Do you have your Halloween costume ready yet?" Amy asked as they went upstairs to her bedroom, with Ginger scampering along behind them.

"Almost," Ella said. "Grandma's helping me make it. I'm going as a witch—how about you?"

"I'll show you," Amy said as they entered the bedroom. "Close your eyes while I put it on so that I can surprise you. Ginger, you close your eyes, too. No peeping!"

Ella obediently shut her eyes, but it didn't sound like Ginger had from the way Amy kept giggling. "Hey, you," she said. "Paws off!"

Then Ella heard a zipper being pulled up. "Okay," Amy said. "Ready!"

Ella opened her eyes to see Amy in a velvety black catsuit, with a long black tail attached at the back. Amy got down on all fours and grinned. "And for the finishing touch . . ." she said, slipping a cat mask over her face. "Meow!"

Ginger had been sniffing at the catsuit
with interest, but as soon as Amy put on the
mask and meowed, he shot
backward so fast that he
almost did a somersault.
His green eyes were wide
with shock, and the next
moment he bolted from the room.

Amy and Ella burst out laughing. "Oh,
dear!" Amy spluttered. "Poor Ginger! He
looked like he really thought I was a gigantic
cat! I'd better take it off."

"You look great!" Ella said, still giggling.
"And at least we know it's realistic. I'll go and
find him—make sure he's okay. Ginger!" she
called, walking out of the room.

Ginger was on the landing. He looked
relieved to see Ella and pattered over to her,

pressing himself against her legs. "It's okay," Ella said, scooping him up and petting him. "The big cat's gone now. Don't worry."

Despite Ella's reassuring words, Ginger stiffened in her arms as they went back into the bedroom. He looked around for the big cat, then jumped onto the floor and sniffed all around the bedroom very suspiciously.

Amy was now back in her ordinary clothes and petted him lovingly. "Don't worry," she said. "You're the only cat for me."

Ella smiled as Ginger broke into a loud, rumbling purr and squeezed his eyes shut happily, enjoying being petted. She couldn't help feeling that it must be nice for Ginger, being the only cat in the house. Misty would probably feel *very* jealous of him right now, if she could see him!

Chapter 4

"There!" said Grandma, putting the witch's hat on Ella's head. "What do you think?"

Ella looked at herself in her parents' full-length mirror and grinned. It was Saturday afternoon, and she was all dressed up for the Kitten Club Halloween party. Grandma had made her a dress and cloak from the sparkly black fabric, which Ella

was wearing with some purple-and-black striped tights. Mom had borrowed a long black wig from one of her friends, too, which completely covered Ella's blonde hair, and Ella had bought a large rubbery nose from the costume shop.

"I love it," Ella said, giggling at her reflection. "It doesn't look like me at all. I'm so . . . spooky!"

Her mom smiled. "Give us a witch's cackle," she said.

Ella turned and made a face at them. "Ha ha ha ha HA!" she cackled witchily, and Mom and Grandma both laughed.

"Let me just add the finishing touches with this," her mom said, picking up a brown eyeliner pencil. She leaned close to Ella's face and drew some small brown circles on her chin and by her nose. "There. Warts," she said. "Perfect."

"Look, here's Honey coming to inspect your costume," Grandma said as the inquisitive kitten padded into the room. "What do you think, Honey?"

Honey stopped dead when she saw Ella and gave a surprised-sounding meow, as if she didn't recognize her.

"It's me!" Ella laughed, bending down to pet her. She pulled off her fake nose to show Honey. "Look, silly."

Grandma smiled. "It's a shame you can't take her along with you. Every witch needs her cat, doesn't she?"

"Amy will have to do instead," her mom said. "Now, where did I put those Kitten Club plaques? I'll find them, and then you'd better go."

Ella gave Honey one last pet. "Be good while I'm out," she said. "Be nice to Misty!"

"I'll keep an eye on them," Grandma said. "Project Happy Cats is safe with me!"

Ella's dad dropped her and Mia—who was in a wizard costume, complete with fake beard—

off at Molly's. Their meeting was starting a little later than usual, since Molly's mom had said they could all stay for a party dinner after they'd played some Halloween games. Ella felt jumpy with excitement as they got to Molly's house. It was always so fun to see her Kitten Club friends—but it was even better when there was a party, too!

Molly answered the door . . . and Ella and Mia both burst out laughing when they saw her. Molly was wearing a bright orange dress with green tights, and had a pumpkin mask with triangle-shaped eyeholes and crooked, cut-out teeth. "You're a pumpkin!" Ella cried. "What a cool costume!"

Molly grinned under her mask. "Yours are great, too," she said. "Come on in. The others are in the kitchen with Truffle. She's having a wonderful time playing with Amy's tail."

In Molly's kitchen, there was a ghost (wearing shoes just like Ruby's) and a skeleton (with a laugh just like Lily's) chowing down on cheese and crackers, as well as two cats— one large and suspiciously girl-shaped, and one small tabby one.

"Hi, everyone," Ella said. "Whoa, Lily, you are *bony*, girl! You need to eat more of that cheese!"

Lily—who, as a skeleton, had white bone shapes pinned all over her—laughed. "Don't worry, I'll fill up on the party food later. Or maybe I'll just snack on that big pumpkin behind you if I get really hungry!"

Ella laughed, then put the box of plaques carefully on the table. "I've got a surprise for you all," she said, lifting the lid. "Ta-dah!"

Everyone crowded around as she unpacked the plaques and handed them out. "Ooh! They look great," Mia said, then promptly sneezed three times. "Sorry," she said. "I think this beard must be dusty. Either that or I'm—*achoo!*—getting a cold."

The girls' meeting began as usual with the roll call and their Kitten Club news. Truffle

sat on Amy's lap, happily
purring, and Amy
wound her long
black tail around
her, which made
everyone laugh.

"Truffle, you're
much braver than
Ginger," Amy said. "He
freaked out when he saw me in this costume,
didn't he, Ella?"

"He was terrified," Ella agreed. "But
Truffle doesn't seem bothered one bit. In fact,
I think you're her new best friend, Amy."

"Smokey's made a new friend, too,"
Mia put in. "There's a black-and-white cat
next door, and Smokey thinks she's the best
thing ever! Whenever she comes into our

yard, he gets all excited and starts showing off, running up trees and trying to climb the fence." She laughed. "I think he's a little bit in love with her, actually."

"Aww," Ella said, smiling. "How sweet! There's a cat who lives near us, too—his name is Nero—this great big tom cat. He's a bit of a thug, I think, and Misty and Honey don't like him very much. That's one thing they agree on, at least."

Lily had brought a photo of her kitten, Buster, in the middle of a huge pile of brown and yellow leaves in their backyard, looking

extremely happy. "Buster's had a great time all week chasing the falling leaves. He just loves them!

Every time Mom or Dad try to rake them up, he wants to join in, pouncing on all the stray ones. It's so cute."

"Ziggy likes them, too," Ruby said, lifting off the white sheet that was her ghost costume, and draping it around her shoulders so that she could see her friends better. "Now that he's Mr. Confident about going outside, he charges around like he's insane whenever the wind is blowing the leaves off the trees."

Ella made a face. "Honey's favorite thing to attack is still Misty!" She sighed, propping her chin up in her hand. "Leaves aren't as much fun as Misty's tail."

Molly, who was sitting next to Ella, peered closely at her hand. "Ouch," she said, looking at the scratch. "And who did this?"

"Misty," Ella replied. "I was trying to stop

them from having a fight, and my hand got in the way. I just wish they could be friends!" She made a face. "It was my project this week to try to help them get along—Project Happy Cats, I called it. More like *Scrappy* Cats, unfortunately."

"Oh, no," Amy said sympathetically. "That must be horrible."

Ella nodded. "I keep telling myself that Honey will probably be calmer when she grows up a little, and they'll get along better . . . but I don't know if I can wait that long!"

Chapter 5

Molly's mom came in just then and smiled at them all. "Okay! Shall we play some games?" she asked, putting six apples in a large tub of water. She put the tub in the middle of the table. "Who wants to bob for apples?"

"Me!" all six girls chorused, making Truffle jerk awake in surprise.

"I think I'd better take my nose off for this," Ella added with a chuckle, unhooking the elastic from around the back of her head. "Otherwise I won't get my mouth anywhere near an apple!"

Bobbing for apples was fun . . . but hard work. It took a while for the girls to bite into an apple and bring it up out of the water in their teeth—and they all, Truffle included, managed to get splashed in the process.

Molly's mom had also hung up some marshmallows on strings, which they had to try to eat without using their hands. It was more difficult than it looked, since the marshmallows kept swinging away from them, and Mia's beard ended up getting pretty sticky. Truffle was fascinated by the dangling marshmallows and sat watching them, her blue eyes wide with interest.

Then they went into the living room to play a Haunted House game where the girls took turns being blindfolded—and then the others would try to spook them! It was really nerve-racking, Ella thought, sitting with a blindfold on, while the others made creepy noises behind her, or brushed things against her face to make her jump.

Just as they'd finished the game, there was a loud barking from outside, and the girls heard the front door opening and lots of boisterous voices. "Uh-oh," Molly said. "They're back from soccer. Watch out, Truffle, the boys are home, and so is Harvey."

The living-room door opened and in trotted a big, sandy-colored dog with friendly eyes and a wagging tail. "Hello, Harvey," Lily said, giving him a pat.

Harvey made a rumbling "woof" in his throat when he saw Truffle, as if he were saying hello to her, but Truffle was already running from the room. They heard her cat flap rattle moments later. Molly sighed. "And it's good-bye, Truffle," she said, patting Harvey. "Hello noisy boys and nosy dog."

"Dinner's ready!" called Molly's mom just then.

The Kitten Club girls went into the kitchen to find a wonderfully spooky spread of food. There were witches' fingers (little sausages), blood pizza (cheese and tomato), and trolls' eyeballs (olives), as well as squashed fly treats (chocolate chip cookies) and baby ghosts (meringues).

Molly's brothers were in the kitchen, too, eyeing the party food hungrily. "Hands off, Alfie," Molly's mom said to the tallest of the boys, whose hand was already hovering over the bowl of skin slices (chips). "This is for the girls. You're having yours later. Boys, you're all filthy! Go and get those muddy things off, please."

"Awww, Moooom," Molly's brothers moaned, traipsing out of the room.

"And, Harvey, get your nose out of Truffle's food bowl!" Molly's mom added, shooing him away. "Honestly, boys and dogs!" she said to the girls, rolling her eyes. "They're as greedy as each other!"

"We heard that!" came a shout from the hall.

The food was yummy, and as she went home that night, Ella felt really happy to be a member of Kitten Club. They always did such cool stuff together, and the girls were the nicest friends you could ask for. Now she just had to persuade her *cats* to be friends, too, and everything would be perfect!

Happy Halloween! I just had the BEST time trick-or-treating. Tons of us from our street went out together, all dressed up. Honey even came some of the way with me, just like a real witch's cat!

It was really sad to say good-bye to Grandma earlier—it's been great having her here, and she's really helped me with the cats. And we have school again tomorrow. BOO!

I am going to miss Honey so much.

On Monday morning, Ella looked for Mia on the school playground, but couldn't see her anywhere. Since Kitten Club had started, the girls had gotten to be really good friends,

and by recess, Ella was really missing her.
She found Mia's big sister, Sunita, on the
playground, who explained that Mia had
a bad cold and was staying home. Ella felt
disappointed, especially since their teacher,
Mrs. Andrews, made her and Fiona Walker,
the meanest girl in class, partners for a new
project. Working with Fiona was not at all
fun. "Ella, you're *hopeless*," Fiona kept saying
loudly. "Your spelling is *awful*. Don't you know
anything?"

Ella gritted her teeth and tried not to get
drawn into an argument. All the same, she was
glad when school let out, and Dad was there
to pick up her and Finn. But when they arrived
back at the house, she found that Misty and
Honey were having a big argument of their own
—a hissing, scratching argument on the kitchen
floor!

"Whoa, major battle," Finn said, staring, but
Ella was worried. This was a violent fight even
by Misty and Honey's standards. She hesitated,
wanting to break them up, but not wanting
another scratch for her trouble.

Just then Honey let out a yelp and cowered
away, as if she'd been hurt. As Ella rushed
over, Misty bolted out the cat flap. Ella picked
up Honey, then gave a cry of dismay. "Oh, no!
Look at her face!"

Chapter 6

The twins and their dad peered at poor
Honey, who had a bleeding scratch just
above her eye. "That looks nasty," Dad said.
"I think we should get the vet to check her
out."

Ella felt shaky just looking at the scratch.
If it had been a few millimeters lower,
it could have been Honey's *eye* that was

bleeding. "Honey, you have *got* to stop hassling Misty," she told her kitten as she put her gently into the cat carrier. "I mean it. I know you only want to play, but you've got to leave her alone. Otherwise . . ." She bit her lip, not wanting to think about the "otherwise."

Dad, Ella, and Finn took Honey along to the vet's. Luckily, it wasn't too busy and they could be seen quickly. The vet prescribed some antiseptic cream for Honey's scratch, and said it should heal up without any problems. "How can we stop the cats from fighting?" Ella asked her. She told the vet they'd tried putting a bell on Honey's collar, keeping the

cats apart where possible, and giving Misty extra attention, but that they still weren't getting along.

"You've done all the right things so far," the vet said. "One other thing you could try is squirting water on them when they fight. All cats hate getting wet, and it'll break them up without you having to get scratched, at least. Once you've sprayed them a few times, you never know, they might get the idea that fighting is a bad thing."

"Cool!" Finn said, his eyes lighting up. "I've got a water gun we can use."

Ella rolled her eyes at their dad. What was her brother's *problem*? Still, at least now he was going to help her break up the cat fights. It would be a nice change from him *starting* them half the time. . . .

WEDNESDAY

Honey's eye is better again—phew—but things between her and Misty are as bad as ever. Honey just can't resist pouncing on Misty, and then Misty swipes at her, and they're off again. Finn and I are becoming good shots with the water gun, though, and getting soaked breaks up the fights really quickly. Of course, Mom FREAKED when Finn squirted them in the living room and accidentally drenched the sofa. We've been told (very strictly!) that we are only allowed to use the water gun outside. Oops.

Other good news—Mia was back at school today. THANK GOODNESS! I was getting totally fed up with being stuck with mean Fiona as a partner.

On Thursday after school, Mia came over to Ella's house. It was November now, but it was still nice and sunny out. They put their coats on and took Honey into the yard, making the most of the sun before it started getting dark. "And we can keep her away from Misty out here," Ella said. "Come on, Honey-pie!"

Remembering what Lily and Ruby had said about their kittens loving playing with leaves, Ella scooped up a handful of leaves that had fallen from the birch tree. She let them drift from her hand so that they floated onto the grass in front of Honey.

Honey quivered with excitement. She crouched into a hunting position, wiggled her bottom, and then gave a mighty spring onto the nearest leaf, rolling over onto her side

with it and kicking it with her back legs.

Ella and Mia both giggled. "I love the way they do that," Mia said. "They act like they're lions stalking prey." She grabbed some more leaves and flung them into the air. "Look, Honey. More leaves to catch!"

Soon Honey was having a wonderful time, pouncing on leaf after leaf as if she were on a mission to fight every single one. But all of a sudden, she froze. Her back arched, her fur stood on end, and her tail fluffed up to twice its usual size.

"What's wrong?" Ella asked in surprise. She turned to see what Honey was staring at, and realized why her kitten was so frightened. Nero, the big black tomcat from two doors down, was on the wall that divided Ella's yard from the one next door. "Shoo," Ella said, flapping her hand at him. "Go on, shoo!"

Nero didn't move. He stayed on the wall, his yellow eyes narrowing as he stared at Honey. "I'll get the water gun," Ella decided. "I'll be right back, Mia."

But Finn, seeing Nero through the
kitchen window, had already grabbed the
water gun and was on his way out with
it. "Cat SHOWER!" he yelled, spraying
everything in sight. Within moments, Nero
had vanished back next door, but the girls
were soaked through, and poor little Honey
was drenched, too. With one terrified look
at Finn, she scrambled up the nearest tree,

where she cowered on a branch.

"Finn!" Ella shouted furiously. "Now look what you've done!"

"Honey, come on, it's okay," Mia called, hurrying over to the tree. But Honey wouldn't come to her *or* Ella when they tried to coax her down. In fact, she edged away from them, going higher up in the branches, her eyes wide and fearful.

"Look at her, the poor thing, she's shivering with cold now," Ella said wretchedly. "Honestly, my brother is such an idiot sometimes! Come on, let's go and find Dad. He'll be able to reach her."

Dad managed to get Honey down by standing on a stepladder. The girls took her inside and gently rubbed her with a towel until her fur was dry. But Honey didn't seem her usual bouncy self after her fright, and was clingy and timid for the rest of the day. Ella felt really angry with Finn. So much for him being helpful—by scaring Honey, he'd only made things worse!

Chapter 7

When Ella woke up on Friday, she still felt annoyed by what her brother had done. Why did he have to be so loud and thoughtless all the time? She didn't speak to him at breakfast, or on the way to school.

That morning, Ella's class was busy practicing their presentation for the assembly the following week. They had been learning about the Romans, and their teacher, Mrs. Andrews, had written a short play about a Roman family that they were acting out. Ella had been chosen to play Flavia, one of the family's slaves, and by a stroke of bad luck, Fiona had been picked to play Claudia, the mother—Ella's boss. Unfortunately, being Fiona, she took to the idea of bossing Ella around much too enthusiastically, and couldn't resist changing some of the lines as they rehearsed.

In the first scene, Ella, as the slave girl, had to assist Fiona in putting on her toga. Fiona stuck her nose in the air, rolling her eyes as Ella tried to wind the white sheet over Fiona's school uniform. "Faster, slave girl, come on!" she said. Then she made a face. "Honestly, this slave is useless," she complained. "No wonder nobody else wanted her."

"Hey!" Ella snapped. "Those aren't the right words!"

"Yes, stick to the script, please, Fiona," Mrs. Andrews said, looking up from her page. "Carry on."

After dressing her mistress, Ella-the-slave had to bring in a Roman breakfast. Mia, who was one of the narrators, said, "Roman families would have bread, honey, and fruit for breakfast. Very rich Romans might eat cheese and olives, too. Their slaves would have a meal of bread and water."

"Hurry up, slave girl!" Fiona ordered. "Get a move on!"

"It doesn't say that in the script, Fiona," Mrs. Andrews said sternly. "Do it correctly."

Ella felt herself bristling as she set down the tray of plastic food. Why did Fiona have to be so rude and horrible all the time?

Recess wasn't any better. Fiona kept calling Ella "slave girl" all the time on the playground and giggling with her friends. "Slave girl, come and tie my shoe for me!" she yelled. "Slave girl, come and brush my hair— it got tangled by the wind. *Now*, slave girl, or you'll be fired!"

"Ignore her," muttered Mia.
"She's just showing off."

Ella did her best to
ignore Fiona, but Fiona
seemed to be enjoying
herself too much to
stop. "Hey, slave girl!
What did you bring for lunch today? As your
mistress, I order you to give me any chips or
cookies."

"No way," Ella snapped, feeling like she
was about to lose her temper. "Come on,
Mia, let's go play somewhere else."

"Slave girl, don't make me punish you!"
Fiona taunted. She and her friends were
crowding in around Ella, mean smiles on
their faces. "Remember what happens to bad
slaves? They get beaten, or—"

She broke off suddenly, and Ella saw
that Finn had appeared, his fists clenched.
"Leave Ella alone," he shouted. "I mean it.
If you talk to her like that again, you'll be
sorry."

To Ella's surprise, Fiona turned pale and cast her eyes down. Finn was popular in their grade, and Fiona clearly didn't want to get on the wrong side of him. Finn glanced over at Ella as Fiona shuffled away, followed by her cronies. "Are you all right?" he said.

Ella blinked, feeling taken aback. "Yeah. Thanks," she said after a moment.

"No worries," Finn said gruffly, then went back to playing soccer with his friends.

"Whoa," Mia said with a grin. "That shut Fiona up, didn't it?"

Ella nodded, still a little stunned. It felt different to be grateful to her brother for the first time in a long time. Different—and kind of nice.

After school that day, Ella went up to her bedroom to practice her lines for the assembly. Even though Finn had put a stop to Fiona's meanness, Ella really didn't want to mess up her part and look stupid in front of her. It was hard to concentrate, though, since her gaze kept drifting to the window, where she could see Honey pottering around in the yard. Ella smiled as Honey sharpened her little claws on the apple tree, explored the undergrowth, and patted a tall clump of grass that was moving in the wind.

But her smile vanished as she saw Nero leap onto the dividing wall. Honey looked up and saw Nero, too, and immediately backed off nervously.

Ella banged on the window, hoping to
scare Nero off, but he didn't bat an eyelid.
He jumped down into the yard and padded
toward Honey, his tail swishing menacingly.
Feeling scared for her kitten, Ella jumped up
from her chair and rushed downstairs. Honey
looked so teeny in comparison to Nero. Ella
had to rescue her!

Chapter 8

But when Ella opened the back door, she
realized that someone else had already beaten
her to the rescue mission. Ella watched as
a fast-moving streak of gray fur shot across
the yard . . . and her mouth dropped open as
she saw that it was *Misty*, hurtling to Honey's
defense.

Ella stared, hardly able to believe her eyes,

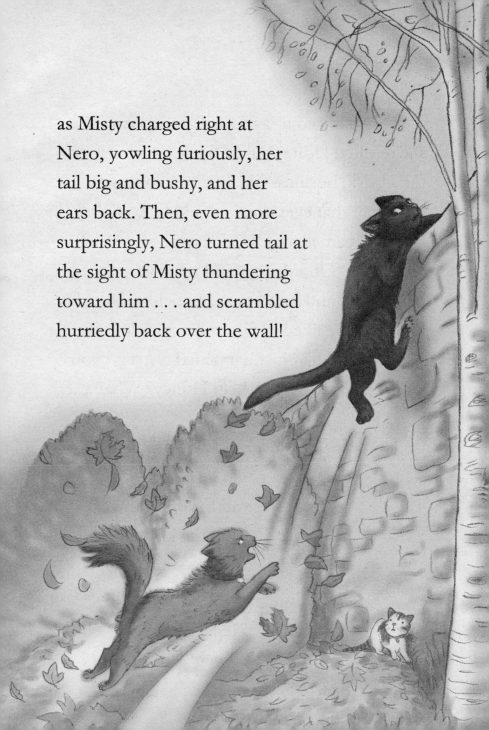

as Misty charged right at
Nero, yowling furiously, her
tail big and bushy, and her
ears back. Then, even more
surprisingly, Nero turned tail at
the sight of Misty thundering
toward him . . . and scrambled
hurriedly back over the wall!

Misty slowed to a more dignified trot as she reached Honey's side. She gave Honey's fur a brisk, business-like lick as if to reassure the kitten that everything would be okay.

Ella beamed and hurried over to pet the brave cat. "Oh, Misty, good job," she said, petting her and scratching her behind the ears just how she liked it. She still couldn't quite believe what had just happened. "Aren't you wonderful, rushing to help Honey? What a good girl!"

Honey came closer to Ella so that she could be petted too, and for once, the cat and the kitten both behaved themselves and allowed Ella to pet them at the same time. Misty purred, and then so did Honey. Ella smiled, feeling very much like purring herself.

The next day was Saturday, and the six friends gathered at Mia's house for their Kitten Club meeting. Everyone loved hearing how Misty had leaped to Honey's defense to shoo away Nero. "It's a little like you and Finn, isn't it?" Mia said with a smile. "You argue most of the time, but then when something serious happens, you stick up for each other."

"I guess so," Ella said. She grinned. "And even though my brother is usually a huge pain in the rear, if a gigantic black cat was about to bully *him*, I think I'd rush to his rescue, just like Misty did." She wrinkled her nose. "Well . . . probably. I might be tempted to turn the water gun on him for a while first, of course."

Everyone laughed. "That's really cool," Lily said. "I guess Misty must feel that Honey's part of the family now."

Ella nodded. "They're never going to be best friends," she said. "And I'm sure they'll still have some fights until Honey gets a little older and calms down. But at least Misty thinks that Honey is worth sticking up for. And feeling like they're both on Team Hughes is definitely a good thing!"

"Hooray for Misty," Ruby said, giggling as Mia's kitten, Smokey, clambered all the way up to her shoulder and began playing with the beads in her braids.

"And I'm glad Honey was okay. Our kittens

have so many adventures, don't they?"

Amy grinned. "Nonstop," she said. "I wonder which kitten will have the next big adventure?"

"Not Smokey, I hope," Mia said, rolling her eyes. "He's already had enough to last him all of his nine lives!"

Just as Mia was saying that, Smokey, who was still playing with Ruby's hair, suddenly lost his balance and tumbled down into Ruby's lap, where he lay blinking up at her and looking surprised. "Oh, Smokey," Ruby laughed, petting him. "You're not supposed to be having any more adventures! Don't you listen to *anything* Mia says?"

Smokey gave a meow as if to say a very bold little "No!" and made a flying leap off Ruby's lap.

"More adventures coming right up," Ella said with a smile as the lively kitten scampered across the room, his bright eyes seeming to search for something new to play with. "But that's why we love our kittens, right?"

"Right!" her friends all chorused as one.

"Meow," went Smokey, as if agreeing, and everyone laughed.

KITTY CORNER

Where kitties get the love they need

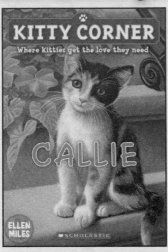

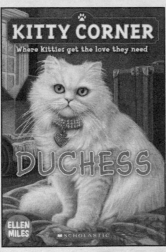

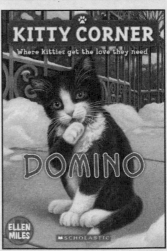

These purr-fect kittens need a home!